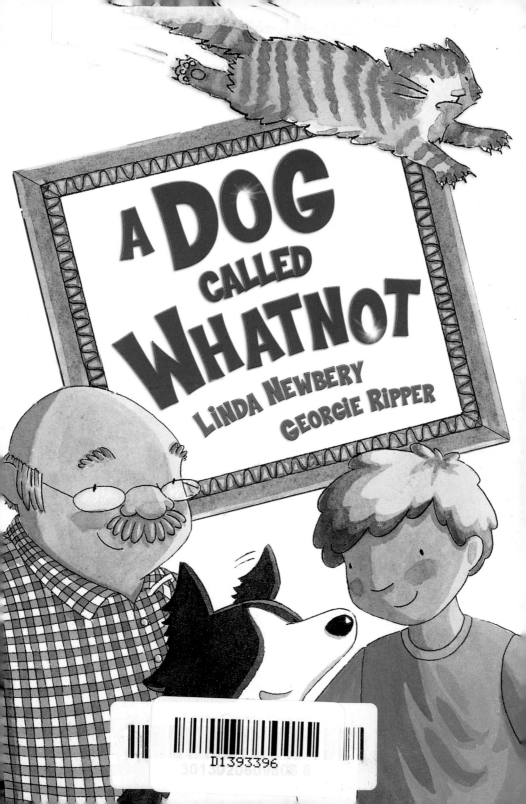

A DOG CALLED WHATNOT

LINDA NEWBERY
GEORGIE RIPPER

For Olivia Hope Bursingham
L.N.
For Dad with love
G.R.

EGMONT
We bring stories to life

Book Band: White

First published in Great Britain 2005
by Egmont UK Ltd
The Yellow Building, 1 Nicholas Road, London W11 4AN
Text copyright © Linda Newbery 2005
Illustrations copyright © Georgie Ripper 2005
The author and illustrator have asserted their moral rights
ISBN 978 1 4052 1204 5
10 9 8 7 6 5 4 3 2 1
www.egmont.co.uk
A CIP catalogue record for this title is available from the British Library.
Printed in Singapore
42487/11

EGMONT LUCKY COIN

Our story began over a century ago, when seventeen-year-old
Egmont Harald Petersen found a coin in the street.

He was on his way to buy a flyswatter, a small hand-operated
printing machine that he then set up in his tiny apartment.

The coin brought him such good luck that today Egmont has
offices in over 30 countries around the world. And that lucky
coin is still kept at the company's head offices in Denmark.

Contents

Lost Dog   5

Louisa the Sneezer   8

Silly Old Whatnot   12

Long and Short   17

Not Very Brave   23

Whatnot Again   29

Cats and Dogs   37

Just Whatnot   43

Red Bananas

LOST DOG

Whatnot arrived in Tim's life one summer
afternoon.

Tim was in the park, playing cricket with
Ajay, when he first saw the dog, watching
from under the slide. It was a young collie,
black-and-white, smiley faced. It watched
keenly, as if wanting to join in. Tim aimed
for the sweatshirt-wicket – Ajay hit the ball
into the bushes, and the dog streaked after it.
He scuffled and he rustled, then burst out
again, carrying the ball in his mouth.

'Hey!' yelled Tim. 'Give it back!'

The dog ran
twice round the
swings before
dropping the ball at
Tim's feet.

'He's better at fielding than you are,' Ajay teased.

The dog waited eagerly for Tim to bowl again, and bounded after Ajay's next shot. His owner would soon whistle him, Tim thought, and take him away. But no one came.

When it was time for home, and Tim and Ajay picked up the sweatshirts and turned for the gates, the dog trotted with them.

'Is he lost?' Ajay wondered. 'He's got no

collar. What shall we do?'

'Better take him home,' Tim said, knowing Grandad would like that.

And not only Grandad. *Tim* would like that. Tim had always wanted a dog of his own – a dog just like this one.

A dog with bright eyes and a laughy mouth.

A dog full of fun and energy.

A dog that would almost talk to him.

come on, boy!

7

LOUISA THE SNEEZER

Tim knew that he'd never be allowed to have
a dog of his own – however hard he promised
to look after it. Mum liked dogs; Louisa liked
dogs; Grandad and Tim *loved* dogs – but there
was a big problem.

Louisa, Tim's sister, was allergic to animal
fur. Flora, her best friend, had two dogs and a
cat, and something about fur made Louisa
wheeze and sneeze. She'd snort and she'd
splutter and her eyes would go teary and
bleary and red. Louisa the Sneezer, Tim
called her. It was so bad that she couldn't go
inside Flora's house but had to wait at the

front door for Flora to come out.

If Tim wanted pets, Mum told him, he'd have to make do with a goldfish.

What use would that be? A goldfish wouldn't be his *friend*.

This dog would. He trotted obediently between Tim and Ajay, pleased and eager. By the time they reached home, Tim never wanted to part with him.

He could be:

A true and close friend.

A warm and furry friend.

A friend who'd always be ready to play
and explore.

A dog with no owner?

A boy with no dog?

Surely *something* could be worked out!

11

SILLY OLD WHATNOT

Grandad and the dog liked each other at once. Grandad found an old tennis ball, and hurled it down the garden. The dog raced wildly after it, and brought it back in his mouth, snuffing and whuffing, smiling his eager-licky smile.

'You're a fine fellow,' Grandad told him, 'a charming chap, a silly old whatnot!'

'I hate to spoil the fun,' Mum said, 'but he can't stay here.'

'Don't take him indoors, or I'll start sneezing.' Louisa was clasping a tissue.

'You'll have to take him to the police station,' said Mum. 'His owner must be worried.'

'But–' Grandad began.

'But couldn't we–' Tim protested.

'To the police station,' Mum said firmly. 'Now. I'll find an old belt for a collar and lead.'

'Oh, just when you've given him such a good name!' said Ajay.

'Name?'

'Whatnot. Silly old Whatnot, you called him. It's just right.'

'*Whatnot! Whatnot!*' Tim tried. The dog cocked his ears and whuffed.

'Name or no name,' Mum said, 'he can't stay here.'

Whatnot thought being on a lead was a new game. He bounced and leaped along the path, he pulled and he tugged, he crossed in front of Tim and back again, tripping him up.

'Come on,' said Grandad. 'Let's get it over with. He must belong to someone.'

'Perhaps they'll give us a reward!' said Ajay.

Whoah!

P'raps there's a reward?

Tim didn't want a reward.

He wanted a dog.

He wanted *this* dog.

LONG AND SHORT

In the High Street, while they waited at the crossing, a big Range Rover pulled up. A row of faces looked out from inside: three humans, and five collie dogs.

A girl inside shouted, 'That's our dog!' All five collies tried to push their noses through the window at the same time, while the woman driver stopped and got out.

Look!
There he is!

'Excuse me,' she told Grandad. 'That's our dog you've got there. Did you find him running loose?'

Grandad explained that they were on their way to the police station.

'We'll save you the trouble,' said the woman. She opened the side door of the Range Rover. All the other dogs tried to surge out, but the children held them back. 'In, Wilmot!' she told Whatnot.

Whatnot pressed himself against Tim's legs.

'Wilmot?' said Grandad. 'We've been calling him Whatnot.'

The woman laughed. 'You weren't far wrong. In you get, Wilmot!' This time Whatnot obeyed, and the other dogs pushed and huffed and panted around him. His owner unbuckled the belt-collar and handed it to Grandad.

'We lost him yesterday. Hates loud noises, he does. Someone fired an air-rifle, up on the common, and he took off.'

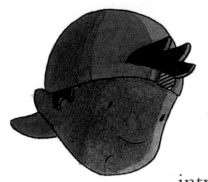

'Is that his family?' Ajay
asked, looking in at the
other dogs.

Whatnot's owner
introduced them

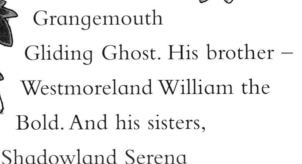

one by one. 'This is his dad –
Battling Braveheart of
Bannockburn. And his

mum –

Grangemouth
Gliding Ghost. His brother –
Westmoreland William the
Bold. And his sisters,
Shadowland Serena
and Sutherland Sophie.

'I'm Fran Mann, and these two are Dan and Jan. Well, we're very grateful to you,' she added, shaking hands with Grandad.

HI!

'Bye-ee!' And she got back into the driver's seat and pulled away. Dan and Jan waved through the window; Whatnot looked wistful.

WOOF 1

Goodbye, Whatnot, Tim thought sadly.

'Fran Mann, Dan Mann and Jan Mann!'
Ajay said. 'They must give the dogs those
long names to make up for having such short
ones themselves. We never asked what
Whatnot's – I mean Wilmot's – full name is.'

'Whatnot,' said Tim. 'That's his name.'

'Don't look so sad, love,' Grandad told him.
'It's all for the best.'

Tim scuffed his shoe.
'He was such a nice
dog. And we'll never
see him again!'

I wanted
him to be
our dog.

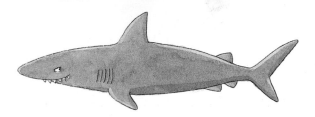

NOT VERY BRAVE

But they did.

Next day, when Tim and Ajay were playing cricket in the park, there was Whatnot again – running in from the bushes, whuffing with delight,

Hey!

It's Whatnot!

snatching up the ball in his mouth and
dashing off again.

'Whatnot!' Tim yelled. Whatnot knew his
name: he bounded up straight away, dropped
the ball at Tim's feet, and dashed round and
round in wild leaps that made Tim dizzy.

'Maybe those Mannses are in the park,'
said Ajay, looking at the swings.

'Or maybe Whatnot got scared again,' said

Tim. 'Or maybe he just likes us!'

They carried on bowling and batting, with Whatnot fielding. When it was time for home, Whatnot knew which way to go.

Ajay used his shorts' belt as a collar and lead. 'This is like a replay of yesterday!'

'Except we know whose dog he is, now,' Tim said.

Maybe *this* time, he thought, it would turn out differently!

Oh!

As they
crossed to
Park Parade,
a big Range Rover
drew up, and out got Fran Mann, on her
own this time.

'Thought I'd find him here!' she
said. 'Come on, Wilmot.' She
gave a little whistle. 'Home.
Car alarm put the wind up
him, this time,' she explained,
while Whatnot slunk into

the car. 'He's the wussiest dog I've ever bred. No courage at all.'

'Good at cricket, though,' Tim said.

Fran Mann drove off, Whatnot looking out of the window until they turned the corner.

Goodbye, Whatnot, Tim thought sadly.

'*I'm* not always brave,' he said to Ajay as they walked towards home.

Ajay thought for a moment. 'You're not scared of dinosaurs. Or man-eating crocodiles.'

'That's only cos I don't meet them very often. I'm scared of – of swimming in the sea, for one thing. Course, I know there won't be sharks or killer whales, but there just *might* be – specially when you start thinking about them. What I mean is, Whatnot's my kind of dog. My kind of dog exactly. But I don't s'pose I'll ever see him again.'

WHATNOT AGAIN

'Have you thought what you'd like for your birthday?' Mum asked. 'It's only two weeks away.'

'I want a dog,' Tim said.

Mum sighed. 'Oh, Tim! We've been through this. You can't have a dog, because of Louisa's allergy.'

'I'm not sure Louisa really *is* allergic to dogs, anyway,' Tim grumped. 'I had dog hair all over my sweatshirt yesterday, and she didn't sneeze once.'

'You think I'm making it up?' shouted Louisa. 'You'd know all right if *your* eyes were red and itchy and you couldn't stop sneezing! Anyway, I *like* dogs!'

Tim went out.
He didn't even feel
like going to the
park today, but he
found himself going
that way, from
habit. Ajay
couldn't play
cricket on his own.

It just wasn't the same
without Whatnot. Tim kept thinking he saw
him out of the corner of his eye – but
once it was a paper bag, once a
duck that had waddled away
from the pond, and
Munch! once a
squirrel eating half
a sandwich.

31

Then, just as they turned for home,
Tim saw Fran Mann and Grandad
outside the park, with Whatnot
on a lead.

There's Whatnot!

The two boys hurried over. 'He must have run off again!' panted Ajay.

Before they reached the park gates, Fran Mann got into her car and drove off, leaving Whatnot with Grandad. As Tim approached, he saw Grandad's face – beaming, grinning, glowing with delight.

'What's going on?' Tim asked.

'Why's she left Whatnot behind?'

Seeing him, Whatnot jumped up at his chest, panting and smiling.

'She's given him to us!' Grandad said, with

the shiniest smile Tim had ever seen.

'But–' said Tim.

'He ran away again today,' Grandad said.
'Brakes squealing frightened him. She's
decided he's too much trouble. Whatnot's the
only one without a special
talent,' he said.

He's ours!

'The others are sheepdogs, or show dogs or
agility dogs. But Whatnot here's no good at
anything. He likes us, and we like *him*, so she
thought we could give him a home.'

'But–' said Tim. Then he stopped Butting. The idea was too much to resist. 'Whatnot! Our dog!' He crouched to make sure Whatnot understood the good news.

'And she told me his real name,' said Grandad. 'It's Wandering Wilmot the Brave.'

'Wandering – yes. Brave – no,' said Tim. 'His name's Whatnot.'

'Haven't you both forgotten something?' asked Ajay. 'You won't be allowed to keep him. What about Louisa the Sneezer?'

CATS AND DOGS

Tim was already beginning to feel sad. It'd be *Goodbye, Whatnot*, yet again!

Grandad looked rueful. 'Well, we can't have young Louisa sneezing all day long. But I couldn't say No, could I? There must be some way round it.'

'What – like Louisa moves out, and Whatnot moves in?' Tim said hopefully.

What about Louisa?

'We could build her a luxury kennel in the garden.'

'Louisa could wear a diving suit and an oxygen tank,' suggested Ajay.

'We'll think of something,' said Grandad.

Whoah!

They were passing Flora's house. There on the front doorstep sat Louisa, with Flora, looking at a magazine; on the gatepost sat Marmite, Flora's tabby cat. Marmite arched her back and hissed at Whatnot – and then everything happened at once.

SLAM!

'TA-RAA, THEN!'
On the other side
of the road, a
delivery man closed
his van door with a
loud **SLAM**. Whatnot
gave a loud **YELP**, turned on
his tail, and set off at a mad
gallop, dragging

Whoah!

Grandad behind him.
'**WHOAH**!' yelled
Grandad. Marmite gave a
piercing **YOWL**, and streaked
towards the open front door of Flora's
house. Flora uttered an ear-splitting
SHRIEK, held out both arms and
got tangled up with the cat.
Louisa breathed in, her
eyes wide.

YOWL!

40

EEEEK!

Tim waited

for it, covering his ears:

'AA – CHOO!
AAAAAA – CHOO!
AAAAAAA – CHOOOO!'

Marmite freed herself and
skitted past into the hall.
Louisa *atish*ooed and *atish*ooed
and a**TISH**ooed. She blinked and bleared
through red teary eyes.

Tim looked down the road, to where
Grandad had managed to stop Whatnot's
wild dash, and was leading him back.

41

Tim thought of the dog-hair-covered sweatshirt he'd left on the back of the sofa last night.

He thought of the dog hairs he'd carefully put on Louisa's pillow last night.

'**CATS!**' he shouted.

Ajay looked astonished. 'What d'you mean, **cats**? There's only one cat, and it's just zoomed off like a ballistic missile!'

'I mean, Louisa's allergic to **cats**! Not dogs! It isn't Flora's **dogs** that set her off, it's Flora's **cat**!'

JUST WHATNOT

Back at home, Mum had to be shown the
Sneeze Test. Louisa – after a bit of persuasion
from Tim - sat on the ground next to Whatnot

Hello,
Whatnot.

and cuddled him, her face close to his fur. Not
a wheeze; not a sneeze; not a wink or a blink.
'So can we keep him?' Tim begged. '*Please!*'

Go on, Mum.

'Well,' said Mum, rubbing her chin. 'A dog needs a lot of looking after, you know! You'll have to take him for walks, even when it's raining, and take him to the vet for injections, and clean up his mess with a Poop-Scoop, and you've got to *love* him, always and always.'

'I'll do all those things!' Tim promised.

'And so will I, when Tim's at school,' added Grandad.

'All right, then,' said Mum. 'We'll keep him.'

I'll help!

Tim ran all the way down the garden and back again, leaping high in the air, with

Whatnot dashing in mad circles around him.

'So,' said Mum, when they were both puffed out. 'What would you like for your birthday?'

Tim thought hard. What more could he wish for, now that his deepest, dearest, most desperate dream had come true?

'I'd like a smart new collar and lead, please,' he said. 'And a name-disc, with Whatnot's name and address on it – just in case he runs off again.'

'He's already got a name-disc. Fran Mann gave it to me.' Grandad delved into his

pocket, and handed the tag to
Tim. 'But it's got his old
name on it.'

*Wandering Wilmot the
Brave,* Tim read.

'That's much too long,'
said Ajay.

'And too silly,' said Tim.

'And only half-true,' added Ajay.

Tim handed the name-tag back to

Grandad. Whatnot wagged his tail and smiled.

'He's our dog now,' said Tim. 'And his name's Whatnot.'

Just WHATNOT.